My Secret Unicorn

A Winter Wish

'There's this clearing I know that's down a hidden path. It's got pink rocks all around it and these amazing purple flowers all over the grass, even in winter,' said Lauren.

'Really?' said Anna.

'Sounds cool!' said Carly. 'Can we go?'

'Well, it's quite a difficult ride . . .' Lauren began. As Carly began to frown, she hastily added, 'But I'm sure you'll be able to manage it . . .'

Other books in the series

THE MAGIC SPELL
DREAMS COME TRUE
FLYING HIGH
STARLIGHT SURPRISE
STRONGER THAN MAGIC
A SPECIAL FRIEND

My Secret Unicorn

Unicorn

A Winter Wish

Linda Chapman

Illustrated by Biz Hull

PUFFIN

PUFFIN BOOKS

Published by the Penguin Group
Penguin Books Ltd, 80 Strand, London WC2R ORL, England
Penguin Group (USA), Inc., 375 Hudson Street, New York, New York 10014, USA
Penguin Books Australia Ltd, 250 Camberwell Road, Camberwell, Victoria 3124, Australia
Penguin Books Canada Ltd, 10 Alcorn Avenue, Toronto, Ontario, Canada M4V 3B2
Penguin Books India (P) Ltd, 11 Community Centre, Panchsheel Park,
New Delhi – 110 017, India
Penguin Group (NZ), cnr Airborne and Rosedale Roads, Albany,
Auckland 1310, New Zealand
Penguin Books (South Africa) (Pty) Ltd, 24 Sturdee Avenue,
Rosebank 2196, South Africa

Penguin Books Ltd, Registered Offices: 80 Strand, London WC2R ORL, England

www.penguin.com

First published 2004

4

Text copyright © Working Partners Ltd, 2004
Illustrations copyright © Biz Hull, 2004
All rights reserved

The moral right of the author and illustrator has been asserted

Set in 14.25/21.5pt Bembo

Made and printed in England by Clays Ltd, St Ives plc

British Library Cataloguing in Publication Data
A CIP catalogue record for this book is available from the British Library

ISBN 0–141–31846–5

To Amany Lily – forever

CHAPTER
One

Lauren stroked Twilight's dapple-grey
neck, her breath misting in the cold
air. 'Almost there.' She spoke softly. Now
that it was December, the woods seemed
very quiet when it started to get dark.

Twilight nodded his head, his bit
jangling. Anyone watching would have
thought he was just an ordinary grey pony
walking down an overgrown woodland

track – but he wasn't. When Lauren said
the words of the Turning Spell, he
transformed into a magical unicorn.

My secret unicorn, Lauren thought, with
a familiar thrill of excitement.

The path came out into a clearing.
Even though it was winter, the short
grass was dotted with star-shaped purple
flowers. Fireflies danced through the still
air, and around the edge of the clearing,
unusual pinky-grey rocks of rose quartz
shone softly in the fading light.

Lauren quickly dismounted. 'We can't
be long. You know Dad gets worried if
I'm out when it's dark. But there's
something I really want to do.'

She took off her hat and, tucking her

long fair hair behind her ears, said the spell that would turn Twilight into his magical form.

'*Twilight Star, Twilight Star,*
Twinkling high above so far.
Shining light, shining bright,
Will you grant my wish tonight?
Let my little horse forlorn
Be at last a unicorn!'

With a purple flash Twilight became a snow-white unicorn. He whinnied and tossed his long mane. His silver horn gleamed.

'Twilight!' Lauren exclaimed, hugging him.

Twilight nuzzled her. 'Hello, Lauren. So, what would you like to do? Don't you want to go flying?'

'Oh yes, of course, but first I want to use your magic to see if Carly and Anna have got the Christmas cards I've sent to them,' Lauren replied. 'I've invited them to come and stay during the holidays.'

Carly and Anna had been Lauren's best friends when she lived in the city. Although she'd kept in touch with them by phone, she hadn't seen them for eight months – not since her family had moved to the countryside.

'Well, let's have a look,' Twilight said. He bent his head towards one of the rose-quartz rocks. As a unicorn, he had many

magical powers. One of them allowed
him to use the special rocks to see what
was happening elsewhere in the world.

Lauren was about to kneel down to
watch when she suddenly frowned.
'Twilight, you will be all right if we do this,
won't you? I don't want to make you ill.'

Twilight's magical powers were only
supposed to be used for helping people. If
Lauren used them too much just for fun
he became weak and sick.

'I'll be fine,' Twilight reassured her.
'We're only going to have a quick look
and you do want to see your friends.' He
touched his horn to the surface of the
rose quartz. 'Carly and Anna, Lauren's
friends!' he declared.

There was a bright purple flash and a cloud of mist swirled over the rock. As it cleared, the surface of the rock shone and a picture appeared. It was like seeing a reflection in a pool.

'There they are!' Lauren gasped, seeing her friends sitting in Carly's kitchen.

Carly's wavy red hair had been cut short since Lauren had last seen her, but Anna looked just the same with her long black hair tied back in a ponytail. They were talking excitedly and looking at two Christmas cards, handmade with gold and silver glitter. Lauren recognized them as the cards she had sent.

'Your friends look really nice,' Twilight commented. 'Do they like horses as well?'

'Oh yes,' Lauren replied. 'They love them although they don't go for regular riding lessons. Carly knows how to ride a bit because she's had some lessons at summer camp, but Anna's only been on a couple of trail rides.' She leaned closer to the rock, eager to hear what her friends were saying. The faint buzz of Carly and Anna's voices became clearer.

'It'll be so cool!' Carly was saying. 'It'll be really good to see Lauren.'

'And her pony, Twilight,' Anna put in.

Twilight gave a proud nicker.

Carly nodded. 'I'm going to get my mum to call Lauren's mum tonight to arrange it.'

'Me too,' Anna said, her brown eyes shining. 'Let's try and go as soon as school ends for the holidays.'

Lauren sat back and their voices faded to a buzz again. 'They're going to come,' she said happily. It would be fantastic to see them again and she couldn't wait to show off Twilight! 'It's going to be hard not to tell them the truth about you,' she admitted.

She wasn't allowed to tell anyone Twilight's secret — not even her mum and dad. The only two people who did know about him were her friend Michael, who lived in the city and had a unicorn of his own, and Mrs Fontana, the old lady who ran the local bookshop. It had been Mrs Fontana who had told Lauren that all around the world there are unicorns, disguised as small grey ponies, who are each looking for a child to be their special secret unicorn friend. If it hadn't been for Mrs Fontana, Lauren would never have discovered that Twilight was a unicorn in disguise.

Twilight looked thoughtful. 'I know you can't tell Carly and Anna about me, but we can still have lots of fun going for rides together.'

Lauren grinned. 'You're right, Twilight. That will be great!'

'Let's go flying now,' said Twilight.

'You bet!' said Lauren, and she jumped up on to Twilight's back. Taking two strides, he leaped upwards into the sky.

It was dark enough now for them not to be seen. The frosty air stung Lauren's cheeks and she was glad of her thick coat and gloves. Lauren's hair flew out behind her as they glided over the treetops that were dusted with a light, shimmering cover of snow. 'It's beginning to feel really

Christmassy,' she said. 'I can't wait until school breaks up on Friday.'

'Then we'll get to spend lots of time together,' Twilight said happily.

Lauren nodded. 'It'll be so much fun.' She loved the holidays when she could spend hours with Twilight – talking to him, grooming him, riding him and, of course, flying with him at night.

At the edge of the wood, Lauren turned Twilight back into a pony by saying the magical words of the Undoing Spell. As she trotted him up the track that led back to the farm, she saw her dad waiting for her.

'I was just starting to get worried,' Tim Foster said. 'You know I don't like you being out in the dark, Lauren.'

'Sorry, Dad,' Lauren said.

'It's all right,' Mr Foster replied, patting
Twilight. 'Just try to be back a little
earlier in the future. I know you're
sensible but the woods *are* more
dangerous in winter. Snow can fall very
suddenly and if that happened, you might
get lost.'

Lauren nodded. 'I promise I won't stay
out late again and I'll be careful.'

Her dad smiled. 'Good girl.'

Lauren dismounted and stroked
Twilight's neck. She knew her dad was
right – the woods *were* more dangerous
in winter – but she also knew that
Twilight would always look after her.

She led him up to his warm stable and
kissed his nose. 'I always feel safe when
I'm with you,' she told him.

CHAPTER
TWO

'Hey, you two! You'll never guess what,' Lauren gasped, running up to her two school friends, Mel Cassidy and Jessica Parker, the next morning. 'I've got some great news!' She paused to catch her breath.

'Whatever your news is, it's not going to beat mine!' Mel announced. 'My mum's said she'll take us to the Christmas fun show at Fox Run Riding School. I went last year and it was totally brilliant! It's on Christmas Eve. There are no jumping classes or anything like that – just lots of gymkhana games and everyone dresses up their ponies with tinsel.'

'Wow!' Lauren exclaimed, her own news going completely out of her head. 'That sounds great!'

'Mel says you have to go in teams of three people,' Jessica put in. 'We can be a team all together!'

They grinned at each other.

'Let's all practise at my house on Monday,' Mel said.

'Yeah!' Lauren replied. She and Mel lived on neighbouring farms and Jessica

and her step-sister, Samantha, kept Sandy,
their new pony, at Mel's, so it would be
easy to meet up.

Just then the bell rang.

'What were you going to tell us,
Lauren?' Jessica asked as they made their
way to their classroom.

'My friends, Carly and Anna, are
coming to stay in the holidays,' Lauren
said, remembering her own exciting
news. Carly and Anna's parents had
phoned the night before and it was all
arranged. Carly's dad was going to drive

the two girls to the farm on Saturday and Anna's dad was going to collect them on Wednesday morning.

'How long are they staying for?' Mel asked.

'Until Christmas Eve,' Lauren told her. 'But they're going early in the morning so I'll be able to come to the show.' She smiled happily. 'I just know you're going to like them.'

She broke off as the classroom door opened and their teacher walked in. They hastily sat down at their desks and the lesson began.

'So, how was school today?' Mrs Foster asked that afternoon when she collected

Lauren and Max, Lauren's six-year-old brother.

'Hard,' Max sighed deeply. 'We never get to do anything fun any more.'

Lauren grinned at her mum. Now that Max was in his second year at school he was always complaining about how much work he had to do.

'Never mind,' Mrs Foster said. 'It'll be the holidays soon.' She switched on the indicator and pulled off the main road.

'Where are we going?' Lauren asked curiously.

'To Mrs Fontana's bookshop,' her mum replied. 'I want to look for some Christmas presents.'

Lauren was pleased. She loved

Mrs Fontana's old-fashioned shop with its
piles of colourful books. She also loved
seeing Mrs Fontana. *I wonder if I'll get a
chance to talk to her about Twilight,* she
thought.

Mrs Fontana was halfway up a ladder
when they arrived. 'Hello
there,' she called.

'Hi, Mrs Fontana,'
Lauren's mum replied as
Walter, Mrs Fontana's
black-and-white terrier,
scampered over to
them. 'We thought
we'd come in for a
browse.'

'Feel free.'

Mrs Fontana's face creased into a warm smile. 'There are some new pony books in the children's section, Lauren.'

Leaving her mum to look in the cookery section, Lauren headed to the far end of the shop.

Max was busy playing with Walter, and Lauren waited to see if Mrs Fontana would come and find her. Sure enough, a few minutes later, the shop owner came into the children's section. 'How's Twilight?' she asked.

'He's fine,' Lauren replied.

Their eyes met and Mrs Fontana dropped her voice. 'Have you been out flying much?'

'Every night,' Lauren whispered.

Mrs Fontana smiled. 'It should snow properly soon and then you'll really have fun. I remember the first time I flew in the snow. It was wonderful.' For a moment she looked lost in memories. She shook her head and focused on Lauren again. 'Enjoy it,' she said softly. 'I promise you it'll be an experience you won't forget.'

'Lauren!'

Hearing her mum, Lauren quickly turned around. 'Yes?' she said, trying to look as normal as possible.

Mrs Foster came into the children's section. 'Why don't you choose a couple of books for Carly and Anna?'

'OK, thanks. That's a good idea!' Lauren replied.

'Carly and Anna?' Mrs Fontana echoed as Mrs Foster left to go back to the adult section and Lauren started looking at the shelf of pony books.

'They were my best friends when I lived in the city,' Lauren explained. 'They're coming to stay on Saturday and we're going to do loads of Christmassy things.' She felt a rush of excitement. 'I can't wait to see them! We've been friends since we were four.'

'That's good,' Mrs Fontana said. 'Friends are very important.' Her bright blue eyes studied Lauren for a moment. 'All friends – old ones, new ones, special ones, even four-legged ones. They all have a part to play in our lives.'

Lauren wasn't sure what she meant. 'Yes,' she agreed hesitantly.

Mrs Fontana smiled. 'Well, I'm sure you'll have a wonderful time.' She spoke more briskly. 'Now, what sort of books do they like?'

With Mrs Fontana's help, Lauren chose pony stories for Carly and Anna. Mrs Foster paid and then she, Lauren and Max went back out to the car.

As they drove home, her mum put a tape of Christmas songs on. Gazing at the decorated shop fronts flashing by in a festive blur, Lauren felt very happy. With the fun show and her friends' visit to look forward to, this Christmas looked like it was going to be the best she'd ever had!

CHAPTER

Three

B y Friday, Lauren was very excited.
Just one more day and then Carly
and Anna would be here! She'd been
busy planning their visit all week. Each
day they were going to muck out and
ride Twilight in the morning and then in
the afternoon they would clean tack and
ride again. She also wanted to do lots of
Christmas things like baking and making

decorations and Christmas cards.

'I want it to be just perfect,' she told Mel, as they rode through the woods on Friday after school. Jessica wasn't with them because she had gone to stay at her gran's for the night. 'I think we'll have a really horsey day tomorrow,' Lauren continued. 'And we might make some Christmas gingerbread in the afternoon. We can decorate it with −'

'The Christmas candies you bought with your mum,' Mel finished, sounding slightly fed up.

Lauren stared at her friend in surprise, taken aback.

'Sorry,' Mel said quickly. 'I didn't mean to be horrid. It's just, well . . . you have been talking about it quite a lot.'

Lauren realized it was her turn to apologize. 'Sorry. It's just I can't wait to see them. They're my oldest friends!'

'I know,' Mel said.

'I really want you to meet them,' Lauren told her. 'Why don't you come over in the morning, then you can see them as soon as they arrive?'

'OK,' Mel replied.

Lauren smiled happily. She was sure Mel would like Carly and Anna as much as she did. She glanced up the wide sandy track. 'Shall we have a canter?'

'I'll race you to the oak tree,' Mel challenged.

'Come on, Twilight!' gasped Lauren as

Mel's light-grey pony, Shadow, set off.
Twilight didn't need any encouragement.
Plunging forward, he caught up with
Shadow and the two ponies galloped side
by side along the track.

★

That night, Lauren made Twilight's bed especially deep and warm. 'I won't be able to come flying tonight,' she told him. 'I've got to get everything ready for Carly and Anna. You don't mind, do you, boy?'

She wondered if he would be upset, but he just bumped her gently with his nose and Lauren knew it was his way of saying that he understood.

'Lauren!' her mum shouted from the house. 'Supper!'

'Coming!' Lauren called back.

Going up the path to the house, she imagined what Carly and Anna were doing right now. Probably talking on the phone. That's what she would have been doing if she were still living in the city. Lauren smiled. Her life had certainly changed a lot in the last eight months. Back then she had spent her time shopping, playing at friends' houses, going to different classes – riding, gym, swimming. Now that she lived in the country her life was totally different. She spent most of her time with Twilight and she was hardly ever out of her riding clothes.

I wonder what Carly and Anna will think? she wondered.

The following morning, Lauren paced up and down the kitchen. Going to the window she checked the driveway for about the fortieth time. No sign of her friends yet. Carly's dad, who was driving them there, had said they would probably arrive about eleven. But it was quarter past already. Where were they?

'I'm sure they'll be here soon,' Mrs Foster said, joining her at the window. 'Don't worry.'

'I just want them to get here,' Lauren said.

Outside, Max was playing fetch with Buddy, his young Bernese mountain dog. Buddy was gambolling about in the puddles on the drive, his enormous paws splashing muddy water everywhere.

'That dog,' sighed Mrs Foster, shaking her head in affectionate exasperation. 'He seems to get bigger every day!'

'He'll be as big as Twilight soon,' Lauren grinned. She glanced down the driveway. 'Mum!' she gasped. 'They're here!'

A sleek black car drew up in front of the house. Carly and Anna were in the back together, looking out of the window. They waved excitedly as Lauren ran outside.

Carly threw open the car door. 'Hi, Lauren!' she cried.

She was interrupted by a massive *woof* as Buddy bounded towards the car, ears flapping and mouth open.

Carly gasped and slammed the door shut.

Delighted at seeing guests, Buddy
jumped up at the car, standing on his
back legs and peering in at the window.

Lauren saw the alarm on her friends'
faces. 'It's OK. He's just really friendly!'
she cried, hurrying towards the car. 'Get
down, Buddy!' she scolded, grabbing his
collar. She hoped Mr Price, Carly's dad,
wouldn't mind the muddy paw prints
over his smart car.

She struggled to hold on to Buddy's
collar.

'Stop being naughty,' Max said to him.

Just then, Mrs Foster came out of the
house. 'Oh, Buddy!'

Mr Price got out of the car. 'Wow!
That dog looks like a handful. Is he a

guard dog?'

'Guard dog?' Lauren echoed, grinning at her mum.

'This is Max's puppy,' Mrs Foster explained with a smile.

'He's called Buddy,' Max added, going over and ruffling Buddy's ears.

Carly and Anna got out of the car. 'I thought he was going to attack us,' Anna joked.

'Hi, boy,' Carly said to him.

Buddy pulled away from Lauren and trotted over to say hello. Carly reached out to stroke him but then hastily pulled her hand back. 'Yuk! He's all muddy!'

Buddy pushed his head against Carly's blue jeans. 'Oh no, my new jeans! They've

got mud on them now!' she gasped.

Lauren stared at her. Since when had it mattered if jeans got muddy?

'I'm sorry, Carly,' Mrs Foster said, hurrying forward and hauling Buddy away. 'I'll run your jeans through the washing machine later. Now, why don't

you all come inside and Buddy can stay
out here?'

They all trooped towards the house.

'What's that smell?' Anna asked,
wrinkling her nose.

'That's just the pigs,' Mrs Foster told
her. 'They're in the far field but when the
wind is in the wrong direction you get
the occasional whiff of them.'

Anna, Carly and Mr Price exchanged
alarmed glances and hurried inside the
farmhouse.

While the adults had coffee, Lauren
gave her friends a tour of the house.
'This is the lounge and this is the dining
room,' she explained. 'And over here's the
sun room.'

Neither Anna nor Carly spoke. It was as if now the initial excitement of meeting was over, none of them knew quite what to say to each other.

As Lauren led the way upstairs, the awkward silence seemed to lengthen. She began to feel nervous. What if the silence went on and on for the next four days?

She needn't have worried. When they reached her room, Carly and Anna both drew in a breath.

'Wow!' said Carly, looking at the light room with its sloping ceiling, wide window seat and walls covered with posters of ponies. 'This is a really lovely room, Lauren.'

'And look!' Anna said, going to the

window. 'Is that Twilight?'

'Yes,' Lauren replied.

'He's gorgeous,' Carly breathed, joining Anna at the window.

'Can we go and see him, Lauren?' Anna pleaded.

'Oh yes, please,' Carly begged.

Lauren felt a rush of relief. It looked as if her friends were excited to be here after all. She decided to tease them. 'Well,' she said as if she were thinking it over. 'I don't know . . .' She broke off with a squeal as Carly tickled her. 'OK, you can see him! You can see him!'

'Right now?' Carly demanded.

'Right now,' Lauren gasped, trying to escape from Carly's tickling fingers.

Carly grinned and stopped tickling her.
'Come on, then! What are you waiting
for?'

'Come on, yourself,' Lauren retorted,
and together the three of them raced
down the stairs.

CHAPTER
Four

'This is Twilight!' Lauren said proudly.

Hearing their voices, Twilight had come to the gate and now he reached over it, blowing gently on Carly and Anna's hands.

'I can't believe he's yours, Lauren!' Anna gasped, her eyes wide.

Carly stroked his cheek. 'He's so

beautiful!'

'Can we ride him?' Anna asked.

'Of course!' Lauren replied. 'I groomed
him this morning so we can ride straight
away.' She looked at their smart clothes.
'But do you need to get changed first?'

'Yes, we'd better,' Carly agreed. 'I don't
want to get my new jeans dirty – well,
any dirtier than they already are,' she
added ruefully, looking down at the
muddy streaks Buddy had left.

'And I should change my shoes,' Anna said, with a glance at her pink sneakers.

They went inside.

'So, what's school like?' Lauren asked as Carly and Anna unpacked some older clothes. 'How is everyone?'

'The same as always,' Carly replied. 'Daniel Armstrong and Mark Siddons are still driving me crazy. I had to sit next to them this term and they kept kicking my chair and throwing balls of paper at me.'

'So nothing's changed there, then,' Lauren said. 'They are *so* annoying!'

'They're not that bad,' Anna protested. 'I do judo with Daniel now and he can be quite nice.'

'Anna loves Daniel!' Lauren and Carly

said at the same time. They grinned at each other.

'I don't!' Anna cried.

Lauren felt happiness fizz up inside her. It was wonderful being back with her old friends again. As they got changed, they told her all the news. There was hardly a second's pause in the conversation, and it was almost as if they hadn't been away from each other at all.

They ran back to the field and Lauren tacked Twilight up.

Anna tried to help by doing up the bridle, but she fastened the throatlash to the noseband strap.

'That's not quite right, Anna,' Lauren said quickly.

'Oh.' Anna looked flustered.

Lauren did the straps up properly.

'Does this go on like this, Lauren?'
Carly asked, putting the saddlepad on
Twilight's back the wrong way round.

'No, it's backwards,' Lauren told her.
She turned it round and then put
Twilight's saddle on. 'The pad has to pull
up into the gullet of the saddle like this,'
she told them. 'It shouldn't press flat
against his back.'

Anna looked at her. 'You know loads
about horses now, Lauren.'

Lauren was surprised. She hadn't really
thought about it before, but back in the
city she'd only ever ridden a pony in a
riding school and she'd never looked after

one on her own before. She guessed she
had learned a lot since she had got
Twilight.

They took Twilight into the field.
Lauren rode first. 'He's really good,' she
told her friends. She trotted round a few
times and then popped over a small jump
before riding back to the gate.

'Can I have a go?' Anna asked eagerly.
She put on Lauren's hat and mounted,

leaning forward nervously in the saddle.

'Do you want me to lead you?' Lauren asked.

Anna nodded gratefully. 'Yes, please.'

Lauren led Anna around the field. 'Try sitting back a bit,' she suggested. 'It'll feel more comfy.'

Anna eased backwards a few centimetres but still clung on to Twilight's mane. He walked calmly, and gradually Anna started to relax.

'This is fun,' she said after five minutes. 'But I should probably let Carly have a turn now.'

They went back to the gate and Carly and Anna swapped over. Carly looked much more confident although she held her reins tightly. 'I don't need leading,' she told Lauren. 'I'll be fine. I had some more riding lessons when I was at camp this summer.' She kicked Twilight. He jumped forwards and she grabbed the reins even tighter. Twilight threw his head back as the bit banged against his teeth.

'Steady!' Carly's voice rose in alarm.

'You're holding the reins too tightly,' Lauren said.

Carly looked cross. 'You don't have to tell me how to ride, Lauren!' She loosened her hold and Twilight walked forward. But as they rode around the field, Carly's fingers crept up the reins again.

Lauren bit her lip. She knew Carly

hated being corrected but she didn't want Twilight to be unhappy either. To her relief, he seemed to wink as he went past, as if to say, *It's OK, don't worry, I'm fine*.

'He's great!' Carly exclaimed. 'Can I try a trot?'

Lauren nodded and Carly urged Twilight into a trot.

He moved forward smoothly. Carly pulled at his mouth a bit but he didn't seem to care. He trotted around the field, his ears pricked and his tail swinging.

Suddenly there was a whinny behind them. Lauren looked round. Mel was riding towards them on Shadow.

'Mel! Hi!' she called, hurrying towards her. 'Come and meet Carly and Anna.

Carly's riding Twilight, and Anna's by the gate.'

Mel rode over. 'Hi,' she said shyly to Anna.

Anna smiled back. 'Hello.'

Carly trotted up. 'Hi, I'm Carly.'

'I'm Mel,' said Mel. 'I live next door to Lauren.'

'Your pony's lovely,' Anna told her.

Mel smiled. 'Thanks. He's called Shadow.'

Carly frowned. 'That's a weird name for such a light-coloured pony.'

Mel looked taken aback and, not for the first time in her life, Lauren found herself wishing that Carly wasn't always so blunt. 'He's called that because when

he was a foal he was almost black,' she
explained. 'That's right, isn't it, Mel?'

'Yeah.' Mel nodded. 'His coat got
lighter as he got older, you see.'

'It's still kind of weird,' Carly said.

Mel frowned and for a moment she
and Carly stared at each other in an
unfriendly way. Lauren felt alarmed. She
didn't want Carly and Mel to argue! To
her relief, Anna changed the subject.

'So, do you two ride together lots?' she asked Mel.

'Yes,' Mel replied. 'Most days after school and at the weekends we go out on the trails in the woods.'

'The three of us went trail riding for the day last March,' Carly said. 'It was at a stable near my aunt's. It was great, wasn't it, Lauren?'

Lauren nodded. 'Do you remember that water fight we had afterwards?'

'When Anna sat in a bucket!' Carly said, grinning.

'I did not sit in a bucket. I was pushed!' Anna protested, with a smile.

Mel spoke up. 'We had lots of water fights *this* summer. Do you remember,

Lauren, when —'

Carly interrupted her. 'What about that hot-dog fight?' she said, speaking to Lauren. 'In the evening when we were camping in my aunt's yard.'

Lauren grinned. 'Yeah. That was really funny.' She turned to Mel. 'The ketchup went all over the tent walls and Carly's aunt was pretty mad.'

Carly and Anna giggled, but Mel didn't look as if she found it that funny.

'It was a really great weekend,' Carly went on. She started reminding the others about all the other things they'd done together — the barbecue they'd had, the midnight feast, the canoe trip on the creek . . .

'Lauren,' Mel interrupted at last. 'I'm going to go home.'

Lauren was surprised. 'But you haven't been here for long.'

'I . . .' Mel hesitated. 'I said I'd help my mum get lunch ready.'

'Oh,' Lauren said, feeling disappointed. 'Well, Twilight's probably done enough for now. I'll ride back a little way with you to cool him off. Is that OK?' she said to Carly and Anna.

'Sure,' they said.

She swapped with Carly and then she and Mel rode to the gate.

'So?' Lauren asked eagerly. 'What do you think of Carly and Anna?'

'Anna seems OK,' Mel replied

cautiously. 'But Carly's a bit full of herself.'

'That's just how she comes across at first,' Lauren told her. 'She's very nice when you get to know her.'

Mel raised her eyebrows as if she didn't believe her. 'She's not a very good rider. She was pulling Twilight's mouth really hard.'

'She wasn't pulling *really* hard,' Lauren said in surprise. 'And so what if she isn't a good rider? That's only because she hasn't had many lessons. She loves horses, and that's the main thing.'

'Well, I wouldn't let her on Shadow,' Mel declared.

'Twilight didn't mind,' Lauren said defensively.

'I bet he did,' Mel said.

'No, he didn't!'

Mel didn't reply and they rode the rest of the way in silence.

'See you then,' Lauren said, when they reached the gate.

'Yeah, whatever,' Mel muttered and, turning Shadow on to the road, she trotted away without looking back.

CHAPTER
Five

Lauren rode back to the farmhouse feeling confused. Why was Mel in such a bad mood? Trying to forget about it, she untacked Twilight, put him in his stable and went into the house.

Her mum had made a delicious spaghetti bolognese for lunch. Afterwards, Lauren, Carly and Anna helped clear the table.

'What are you three going to do now?'
Mrs Foster asked, as they put the last of
the plates in the dishwasher. 'If you want,
you could make some gingerbread
decorations for the Christmas tree.'

Lauren looked at her friends. 'Well, I
usually skip Twilight's stable out after
lunch. Shall we go and do that first?'

'Skip his stable out?' Anna said. 'What
does that mean?'

'Take out the dirty straw,' Lauren
explained.

Carly frowned. 'But it's raining.'

Lauren glanced out of the window. It
was drizzling just slightly. 'Only a bit and
we'll be inside the stable.'

'Let's do it **later**,' Carly said. 'I'd like to

make decorations.'

Lauren gave in. 'OK.'

'You can decorate the shapes with white icing,' Mrs Foster said as she got out the pastry cutters. 'Max, do you want to come and help?'

It was great fun. Even Buddy tried to join in. He sat with his big nose right up to the table top, his dark eyes following them as they rolled and cut the gingerbread into stars, holly leaves and candles.

'No, Buddy!' Lauren said quickly when she saw him licking his lips and eyeing a nearby star. 'These aren't for you to eat.' She cut out the last shape. 'All finished,' she declared. 'Now they just need to bake.'

After the gingerbread had baked and cooled down, they decorated it with white icing and silver sugar balls.

'Right, we'll let them dry now,' Mrs Foster said. 'And then we can put some ribbon through them and hang them on the Christmas tree.'

'Let's go and skip out,' Lauren said to Carly and Anna.

Anna looked out of the window at the grey skies. 'It looks really cold.'

'It won't be when we're in the stable,' Lauren told her. 'Come on!'

They pulled on their boots and coats and went outside.

Because Twilight hadn't been skipped out earlier his bed was messier than usual.

Lauren fetched the wheelbarrow, three forks, a spade and a brush. 'I think we'd better muck him out properly so his bed will be nice and clean this evening,' she told Carly and Anna.

Carly picked up a fork. 'OK. What do we have to do?'

'The dirty straw goes in the wheelbarrow,' Lauren explained. 'And the clean straw goes against the wall of his stable. Like this.' She showed them how to use a fork to shake the clean and dirty straw apart.

'Ew!' Anna said. 'It smells terrible!'

Carly cautiously shook a forkful of straw. Some dirty straw fell on her glove. 'Yuk!' she exclaimed, shaking it off.

Anna poked at a pile of straw with a fork. 'I think this bit is clean over here,' she announced.

Carly giggled. 'I'll do that bit then.' She attempted to throw the clean straw into the pile against the wall, but she picked up too much on her fork and it scattered all over the bed, mixing in with the droppings. 'Whoops!' she said. 'Sorry!'

Lauren began to think it would be far quicker to muck out on her own! 'Look, maybe it would be best if I did this while you fetched some more clean straw,' she suggested. 'It's in the barn over there. Would you mind bringing me about five slices in a wheelbarrow?'

Carly and Anna nodded and went to

the barn. They returned five minutes later
with a laden wheelbarrow.

'Here we are!' Carly said cheerfully.
'We've got the straw!'

Lauren looked at the barrow. 'That's
hay, not straw.'

'Oh,' Anna said, her face falling.

'Sorry, Lauren,' Carly said.

'It doesn't matter,' Lauren sighed. 'I'll go and get some more.'

Looking as if they didn't really know what to do, Carly and Anna watched as she fetched some straw and spread it over the bed.

'Do you have to do this every day?' Anna asked.

Lauren nodded.

'Rather you than me,' Carly commented.

'Yeah,' Anna agreed, shivering. 'It's freezing out here!'

Lauren felt guilty. It was clear that neither Anna nor Carly were enjoying mucking out. She hurried through the chores. Soon the stable was finished and Lauren brought Twilight in from the field.

''Night, boy,' she said, rubbing Twilight's nose. *See you later on*, she thought.

Twilight looked at her and Lauren was sure he was thinking the same thing.

'Come on, Lauren, let's go in!' Anna urged.

Lauren shut Twilight's door.

'So, what are we going to do tonight?' Carly said as they took their boots off in the porch. Her eyes lit up. 'I know, why don't we have a midnight feast?'

'Yeah!' Anna said. 'We've brought loads of sweets with us.'

'OK,' Lauren agreed. 'But can we have

it earlier than midnight? I have to get up to feed Twilight in the morning.' *I wanted to take Twilight flying tonight, but I won't be able to if Carly and Anna are still awake!* she thought.

'But it won't be a midnight feast if we don't have it at midnight,' Carly protested. 'We can't have it earlier.'

Lauren didn't want to seem like a spoilsport, and she really loved the idea of having a proper midnight feast. She thought quickly. She was sure Twilight wouldn't mind if she missed flying that night. 'OK, midnight's fine,' she agreed.

'Cool!' Anna said.

'So what sweets have you got?' Lauren asked.

'All sorts,' Carly told her. 'Let's go to your room and we'll show you.'

'OK,' Lauren agreed happily, and they all hurried upstairs.

CHAPTER
Six

When Lauren's alarm clock went off the next morning, she felt so tired that she could hardly drag herself out of bed. She and Carly and Anna had stayed awake talking and eating sweets until almost two o'clock in the morning.

'What time is it?' Carly murmured sleepily as Lauren tried to find her jeans.

'Quarter to seven. I've got to feed

Twilight,' Lauren yawned.

'What, now?' Carly said. 'Go back to bed. He won't mind waiting.'

But, tired as she was, Lauren knew there was no way she could go back to bed, knowing Twilight was waiting for his breakfast.

Leaving Carly and Anna to go back to sleep, she went downstairs. A heavy frost had fallen in the night – so heavy that Lauren left footprints in it as she trudged down the path to Twilight's stable. He whinnied when he saw her.

'I'm really sorry I didn't come out last night,' she told him, going into the stable and putting her arms around his neck. 'Carly and Anna wanted to have a midnight feast.' She bit her lip. 'Actually I think it's going to be too risky to try and come flying while they're sharing a room with me. What if they wake up and find I'm gone?'

Twilight stared at her.

Lauren wished she could turn him into a unicorn so she could talk properly to him. 'I'm not sure what to do,' she told him. 'I know you love flying, but I just don't know if I should risk it.'

Twilight lifted his muzzle to her face and blew out gently.

'Are you trying to say it's OK?' Lauren asked.

Twilight nodded.

Lauren rested her forehead against his.

'Thanks, Twilight.
We'll be able to
go flying
again soon. I
promise.'

Twilight stamped his hoof. Lauren took
the hint. 'All right. You're hungry. I'll go
and get your breakfast.'

Fifteen minutes later, leaving Twilight
with some fresh water and a big hay net
to munch, Lauren went back to the
house. It was almost nine o'clock before
Carly and Anna got up.

'I can't believe you have to get up so
early every day, even during the holidays,'
Carly yawned as she pulled on her
clothes.

'You used to hate getting up early,' Anna said.

Lauren shrugged. 'It's just one of those things you have to do when you've got a pony.'

After breakfast they went outside. Remembering the day before, Lauren decided it might be easier if Carly and Anna groomed Twilight while she mucked out. That way they didn't have to get dirty.

'We don't mind helping you muck out,' Anna said, when Lauren told them her plan.

'Really,' Carly said. 'It was fun yesterday.'

'It's OK,' Lauren replied hastily, sure

that they were only offering because they were being polite. 'It'll be quicker if I do it. At least I know the difference between hay and straw,' she tried to joke.

Unfortunately, Carly and Anna didn't seem to think it was funny. They both looked quite hurt.

'We didn't mean to get it wrong yesterday,' Carly said.

'We just didn't know,' Anna put in.

'Yeah, we're not all lucky enough to have ponies of our own,' Carly said.

'I know. I'm sorry,' Lauren apologized. 'I didn't mean it like that.'

'Are you sure you can *trust* us to groom Twilight?' Carly said sarcastically.

'Of course I can,' Lauren said. 'And you

can help me muck out if you really want.'

'No, no, it's obvious we don't know enough,' Carly retorted.

Lauren knew that when Carly was in this sort of mood it was best just to ignore her so, giving Anna and Carly the grooming kit, she started the mucking out. Luckily by the time they took Twilight into the field, Carly's bad mood seemed to have lifted.

They took it in turns to ride Twilight. Anna was still nervous but Carly was growing in confidence. She cantered Twilight twice round the field and, although she lost her stirrup and had to hang on to his mane, she seemed delighted to have gone so fast.

'Can I try jumping him?' she asked eagerly.

Lauren hesitated. She knew the only reason Carly had stayed on was because Twilight was being so well-behaved. 'Maybe tomorrow. Twilight's done enough today.'

'OK,' Carly agreed reluctantly.

They untacked Twilight and went inside.

Lauren's dad was making a cup of coffee. 'Lauren, Mel rang while you were with Twilight. She asked if you could call her back.'

Lauren nodded. She was about to pick up the phone when she remembered the bad mood Mel had been in the day before. Maybe she'd ring her later, she decided.

'So what are we going to do now?' Carly asked.

'I don't know,' Lauren answered. 'We could play with my model horses or read pony magazines?' She and Mel often did things like that when they were inside. But neither Anna nor Carly looked that keen.

'Couldn't we go out or something?' Carly suggested.

Just then, Mr Foster spoke. 'How about we take a trip into town? There's a Christmas market being held in the main street today.'

'That sounds cool!' Carly said.

Anna nodded. 'I've brought some money with me. I can buy some presents to take home.'

'Me too,' Carly put in.

'OK,' Lauren said. 'Can we go, Dad?'

'Sure,' Mr Foster said. 'I'll go and tell your mum and Max while you three get your coats.'

Half an hour later, Mr Foster parked the car in a side street in town. Lauren piled out with Carly, Anna and Max. The cold air was filled with the smell of roasting chestnuts. 'Doesn't it smell Christmassy!' Lauren exclaimed.

'Yeah. Where are the stalls?' Carly asked, looking around.

'In the main street,' Mrs Foster said. 'It's this way.'

They headed into the town centre. There were people everywhere, bustling along with bags and shopping baskets, and Christmas music was playing in every shop they passed. Lauren felt happiness bubbling inside her. Christmas suddenly felt very close!

'Brr, it's cold,' Anna said, pulling her coat around her.

'At least it's not raining,' Mrs Foster said.

But she spoke too soon. Just then, a raindrop spattered against Lauren's sleeve.

'Maybe I shouldn't have said anything,' Mrs Foster said ruefully. 'Hopefully it's

just a passing shower. Come on, let's
hurry!'

To everyone's relief, by the time they
reached the main street the rain had
stopped. A very Christmassy scene
greeted them. There were about thirty
stalls selling everything from wreaths to
home-made stockings. A group of
Christmas carollers was singing round a
small platform and a man was roasting
chestnuts nearby. Lauren looked around
excitedly. There were so many things
to see.

Max pointed to the end of the street
where a large Christmas tree was
towering up into the sky. It was
decorated with silver and gold lights.

'Wow! Look at that Christmas tree! It's huge!'

Carly looked at it and shrugged her shoulders. 'That's nothing compared to the one they've got back at home. It's about twice as tall and it's got loads more lights on it, hasn't it, Anna?'

Anna nodded. 'Yeah, it's much bigger.' She looked around. 'There aren't many stalls, are there? I thought it would be a really big market.'

She sounded disappointed, and Lauren felt her excitement dampen slightly. Her friends didn't seem very impressed with the market.

'Well, I'm sure you'll find some things you want to buy,' Mrs Foster told them.

'Now, why don't you three go and have a look around on your own? We'll meet you by the Christmas tree in forty minutes. Then we can get some hot cider and Christmas cookies.'

Lauren, Anna and Carly set off. To Lauren's relief, her friends seemed to cheer up as they started to look at the different things.

'Look at these!' Anna said, dragging Lauren over to look at a stall that was selling beautifully iced gingerbread houses. 'I bet my mum would like one. She loves gingerbread and these are really pretty.'

'And there's a place over there selling salt-dough decorations,' Carly said. 'My gran loves those. I could buy her something to put on her Christmas tree.'

Lauren had her eye on a stall that was selling home-made sweets. 'I want to go over there,' she said. 'Those sweets look delicious!'

It didn't take them long at all to spend their money!

'What shall we do now?' Carly asked. She looked at her watch. 'We're not meeting your mum and dad for another ten minutes.'

Just then it started to rain again.

'Let's go and wait over there,' Lauren said, pointing to a shop doorway near the Christmas tree. 'At least we'll be out of the rain.' The others nodded but by the time they reached the doorway, it was already full of other people who had had the same idea.

The three girls stood against the wall of the building. It sheltered them slightly from the rain but not from the cold.

'I'm freezing!' Carly shivered.

'Me too!' Anna agreed. 'I hope your

mum and dad come soon, Lauren.'

Lauren hoped so too. Her hands and feet were cold and now that the excitement of shopping was over she felt suddenly tired. Her late night and early morning start were catching up with her.

It began to rain more heavily. 'This is horrid,' Carly complained as raindrops splashed on her coat.

'I want to go back to the farm,' Anna

said. She and Carly huddled together.

Lauren scanned the street. Where were her mum and dad and Max? *Come on*, she thought, looking guiltily at her unhappy friends. *Please hurry up!*

Just then her dad came hurrying through the crowd. He had a large umbrella with him.

'Dad!' Lauren called in relief.

Mr Foster came rushing over. 'There you are!' he said. 'Get under here before you get any wetter.'

The three girls quickly joined him. 'Where are Mum and Max?' Lauren asked.

'They've gone back to the car,' Mr Foster replied. 'It looks like we're going

to have to abandon this shopping trip,
I'm afraid.'

Anna nodded. 'I'm really cold.'

'Come on then,' Mr Foster said. 'Let's
go home.'

It was a relief to get back into the car.
Mrs Foster had the engine running and
the heater on.

'Well, that was a bit of a washout,' she
said, looking over her shoulder as they set
off for the farm. 'Sorry about that, girls.'

'It's OK,' Carly said, looking happier
now she was in the warm car. 'At least we
got some shopping done.'

'Yeah, I bought a gingerbread house for
my mum and some sweets,' Anna put in.

'And it was fun until it started raining,' Carly said.

Despite her friends' upbeat words, Lauren couldn't help still feeling guilty. She was sure they hadn't really enjoyed the market. She bit her lip. Carly and Anna's stay wasn't turning out like she'd expected at all. She'd wanted them to have a really good time while they were staying with her, but everything just kept going wrong.

Carly turned to her. 'What are we going to do tomorrow, Lauren?'

'I don't know,' Lauren replied in a subdued voice.

'Well, what do you normally during the holidays and weekends?' Anna asked.

Lauren shrugged. 'Things with Twilight – rides in the woods.'

Carly frowned. 'That sounds a bit boring.'

'It isn't,' Lauren protested. 'The woods are great.' As she spoke, she had an idea. Why didn't she take Carly and Anna to the secret clearing? It was an amazing place even if she couldn't tell them it was magic. 'There's loads to see in the woods. Like this clearing I know that's down a hidden path. It's got pink rocks all around it and these amazing purple flowers all over the grass, even in winter.'

'Really?' said Anna, looking interested.

Lauren nodded. 'In the evening there are hundreds of fireflies and in the summer there are butterflies everywhere.'

'It sounds cool!' said Carly. 'Can we go?'

'Well, it's quite a difficult ride . . .' Lauren began. As Carly began to frown, she hastily added, 'But I'm sure you'll be able to manage it. We can go tomorrow if you like.'

Carly and Anna nodded eagerly.

As Lauren watched the houses flashing past, she thought about taking Anna and Carly to the clearing. No one knew about it – not even Mel. She felt a flicker of nervousness. She just hoped Carly and Anna liked it enough to see that staying in the country with her really was fun after all.

★   ★

CHAPTER
Seven

W hen Lauren came in from feeding Twilight the following morning, the phone was ringing. It was Jessica.

'Hi, Lauren. I . . . um . . . well, I was just wondering if you were still coming over to Mel's this morning.' Jessica sounded uncomfortable.

'To Mel's?' Lauren frowned.

'To practise for the show. We arranged it last week.'

Lauren's eyes widened. She'd completely forgotten that they'd agreed to have a practice that day.

'Mel said she called yesterday to remind you but you didn't ring her back.' Jessica hesitated. 'I . . . I think she's a bit upset, Lauren.'

Lauren felt guilty. She'd been so busy with Carly and Anna that Mel's phone message had slipped out of her mind. 'It was just a mistake,' she said quickly.

'Well, are you coming today?' Jess asked.

Lauren felt torn. What about Carly and Anna? They were expecting to go to the secret glade in the woods. 'I don't know. It's difficult because of Carly and Anna, but I'll try my best to come.'

'OK,' Jessica said slowly. 'Well, I guess I might see you later.'

Lauren put the phone down. What was she going to do?

Mrs Foster came into the kitchen. 'Is everything OK?' she asked, seeing Lauren's worried face.

Sitting down at the kitchen table, Lauren told her about the mix-up.

'Well, can't Carly and Anna come to Mel's with you?' her mum asked.

'I don't think Mel likes Carly very much,' Lauren said, and she told her mum about Mel's bad mood on Saturday.

Mrs Foster sighed. 'Oh dear. I see.'

'What should I do, Mum?' Lauren asked.

'I think you should probably go to Mel's house,' Mrs Foster replied. 'It sounds to me as if Mel might be feeling a bit left out because of you having Carly and Anna here, and I'm sure they won't mind if you're only gone for a few hours. Wait till they wake up and then see what they say.'

Carly and Anna seemed a bit surprised when they came downstairs and Lauren said she had to go over to Mel's to practise for the show.

'But you said we could go to that clearing in the woods!' Carly protested.

'I'm really sorry,' Lauren told her. 'I'd forgotten all about this practice. We're doing all sorts of pony races on Wednesday – sack race, egg and spoon . . .'

'Can we come and watch you practise?' Anna asked.

'Yeah, it sounds fun,' Carly agreed. 'We could help you set everything out.'

Lauren felt alarmed. How would Mel react if she brought Carly and Anna? Lauren was sure she wouldn't be too happy. 'You wouldn't know what to do,' she said quickly.

'Well, you could tell us,' Carly replied.

'It'll just waste time if we have to stop and explain everything,' Lauren told her.

Carly frowned. 'It can't be that hard.'

To Lauren's relief, her mum spoke. 'I

think it might be best if you stay here, Carly. It's so cold today. You'll freeze if you're standing around waiting to have a ride. Why don't you and Anna stay and help me ice the Christmas cake instead?'

'I love icing Christmas cakes,' Anna said.

Carly hesitated. 'OK, we'll stay,' she agreed, shooting Lauren a cross look.

Lauren sighed. She seemed to be annoying *all* her friends at the moment!

★

Riding up the drive to Mel's house later that morning, Lauren felt nervous. What sort of mood would Mel be in? She was obviously fed up that Lauren hadn't phoned her back the day before.

'Hi,' Lauren called as she rode over to the field gate.

Mel and Jessica were cantering around the field on Shadow and Sandy. They slowed down and rode over to meet her.

Jessica smiled. 'Hi, Lauren.'

Mel didn't say anything.

Lauren felt awful. She'd never fallen out with Mel before and she didn't like it. 'Sorry I didn't ring you back yesterday, Mel.'

'Yeah, well, I guess you forgot,' Mel said coldly.

'It's just that we all went out a–and . . .' Lauren stammered.

'Whatever,' Mel interrupted. 'It doesn't matter.'

There was a moment's silence.

'Well, should we start to practise then?' Jessica said quickly. 'How about we start with a bending race?'

'Great,' Lauren said. 'But I can't stay too long. I've got to get back to –'

'Carly and Anna,' Mel finished. 'You don't have to be here at all if you don't want to be, Lauren.'

'I *do* want to be here!' Lauren protested.

Mel raised her eyebrows. Lauren felt herself starting to get cross. She'd said she was sorry about not phoning her. What else could she do? She frowned and opened her mouth, but before she could say anything, Jessica spoke up. 'Come on, let's start!'

Lauren kept silent.

They rode over to where there were three buckets and, a little way off, three barrels with a pile of potatoes on.

'We have to gallop up and get a potato, then gallop back and throw it into the bucket,' Jessica said. 'Ready, steady, go!'

The three ponies surged forward, but Lauren's mind wasn't on the game and it seemed like Mel's wasn't either. Both of them missed the bucket and Jessica was easily the winner.

The sack race was no better. Shadow galloped straight past the sack and Lauren fell over.

The other races went just as badly. The final straw came when Lauren tripped over Twilight's legs in the walk, gallop and lead, making Shadow pull back in alarm. Mel lost her grip on his reins and he trotted off around the field, refusing to be caught for ten minutes.

When Mel finally did catch him, Jessica looked at her and Lauren in exasperation. 'We're going to do dreadfully on Wednesday if we're as bad as this.'

'Well, maybe if Lauren could stop

falling over it would help,' Mel frowned.

'And maybe if you could hang on to
your reins then we wouldn't have to spend
so much time catching Shadow,' Lauren
retorted. She was freezing cold from
standing around and totally fed up. She'd
upset Carly already by coming over. The
last thing she needed was Mel sniping at
her too. 'I'm going home,' she said.

'But, Lauren, what about the practice?'

Jessica protested.

'It's too cold,' Lauren said. 'I'll see you on Wednesday.' And before Jessica could say anything more, she turned and rode Twilight away.

As she rode him along the road, she felt her anger die down. She shouldn't really have left like that but she'd been feeling so fed up with Mel.

'Oh, Twilight,' she sighed, stroking his neck. 'What am I going to do?' More than anything she wanted to turn him into a unicorn.

She saw a dense copse of trees at the edge of the road and decided to risk it. Riding him into the trees, she checked there was no one around and said the magic spell. With a flash, Twilight turned into a unicorn.

Lauren hugged him.

'You're not having a good day, are you?' he said, nuzzling her.

'No,' she replied. 'Everyone's cross with me, Twilight. The practice was awful. I don't know what to do.'

'Me neither,' Twilight admitted. 'I don't think they're the sort of problems my magic can solve.'

Lauren leaned her head against his neck. Just talking to him had made her feel a bit better. 'I should turn you back,' she said reluctantly. 'Someone might come along.'

Twilight nodded. 'Things will get

better, Lauren. I'm sure they will.'

Lauren hoped he was right. Saying the Undoing Spell, she turned him back into a pony.

'Come on,' she said with a sigh. 'Let's go home.'

CHAPTER

Eight

'Hi,' Lauren called, going into the kitchen. Carly and Anna were just cleaning up after icing the Christmas cake. 'The cake looks great,' Lauren said, admiring the huge cake with crisp snowy peaks of white icing. It was decorated with plastic robins and snowmen.

'Thanks,' Anna said. 'We helped your mum make some muffins too,' she said, pointing to a tray of sweet-smelling muffins on the side. 'How was your practice?'

'Oh, OK,' said Lauren, not wanting to talk about it. She glanced at Carly who was screwing the lid on the tin of icing sugar. 'I'm sorry I had to go off like that,' she apologized. 'What would you like to do this afternoon? We can do anything you like.'

Carly looked up. 'Can we ride Twilight in the woods?'

'Yes, can we go to that clearing?' Anna asked. 'The one you told us about?'

'Sure,' Lauren agreed. 'We'll go this afternoon.'

★

But when they went outside to
Twilight's field after lunch, the clouds
overhead looked heavy and the air
seemed strangely still and quiet.

'I think it's going to snow,' Lauren said,
her breath coming out in a cloud. 'We'd
better not go to the woods, after all.'

'Why not?' said Carly.

'It'll be too dangerous if it snows,'
Lauren explained. 'The paths will get

slippery and if there's a blizzard we might get lost.'

Carly looked at the sky. 'It's not going to snow. It's just cold, that's all. Come on, let's go.'

'No,' Lauren said. 'It's too dangerous.'

Carly frowned. 'I bet you're just saying it's going to snow because you think we're not good enough to go riding in the woods.'

'Of course I don't think that . . .' Lauren started to protest, but just then her dad drove up in his Land Rover, with the livestock trailer bumping along behind.

'Lauren!' he called. 'Are you free? I have to go to the East Hill field and bring in the four ewes who are about to lamb. I don't want them cut off on the hillside if it starts to snow. Do you think you could come and help me?'

'Of course,' Lauren said. She looked uncertainly at the others.

'It's OK, we can ride later,' Anna said. 'Come on, let's go and help your dad.'

Lauren thought for a moment. The East Hill field was really muddy and cold. She was sure Carly and Anna would hate it. 'You don't have to come. You could stay and ride in Twilight's field. I don't mind going with Dad on my own.'

'But we might be able to help,' Carly said.

Lauren remembered the last time she had helped her dad round up sheep. She had ended up splattered in mud from head to toe. 'No, really,' she insisted. 'You stay. Dad and I will manage fine.'

'Surely it'll be easier with four of us?' Carly pointed out.

'You won't know what to do,' Lauren said as her dad pipped his horn.

'Lauren, we're not totally useless, you know,' Carly said, sounding exasperated.

Mr Foster pipped his horn again.

'Look, don't worry about it,' Lauren said hastily, and she hurried over to the gate.

As she got into the Land Rover, she glanced back. Carly and Anna both looked upset and cross. Lauren's heart sank. She'd meant to save them from doing something they wouldn't enjoy, but it just looked like she'd hurt their feelings. She pushed her hands through her hair. She'd never thought having her friends to stay would be so stressful!

As Lauren helped her dad round up the sheep and put them in the back of the vehicle, she thought about Carly and Anna. She hoped they were having a good time riding Twilight.

It was cold on the hillside and as Mr Foster caught the last sheep it started to snow.

Within minutes the flakes were falling thick and fast.

'Looks like we got here just in time,' said her dad. He nudged the sheep up the

ramp of the trailer. 'Come on, let's get
back to the farm.'

As they bumped down the rough track,
Lauren watched the fields turning white.
She hoped Carly and Anna had
remembered to untack Twilight and put
his rug on.

Mr Foster stopped the Land Rover by
Twilight's stable. 'You get the others and

hurry into the house,' he said. 'I'll just drop the ewes off in the lower paddock.'

Lauren nodded and got out. Her dad drove off and she went to Twilight's stable. She looked over the door. 'Hi.' She stopped. The stable was empty!

She stared around. Where were Carly and Anna? Where was Twilight?

She hurried to the tackroom. There was no sign of her friends but there was a note on the table.

Dear Lauren

We're bored of riding in the field so we're going to the woods. Don't worry! We're not

totally useless. We'll be fine.
Lots of love,

Carly and Anna xxx

Lauren stared at the note. Carly and Anna had gone into the woods, even though she had told them not to! What if they couldn't find the way home in the snow, or Twilight slipped and hurt himself? They'd be stuck outside in the freezing cold. Lauren's heart pounded.

What was she going to do?

CHAPTER

Nine

L auren stood in the doorway to the
tack room. The snow was falling
thick and fast now. Her dad was down in
the lower pastures with the sheep and her
mum was in town with Max. She didn't
even have Twilight.

I've got to go after them, she thought. *I
need to make sure they're OK.*

Even as she thought it, she realized it

would be stupid to go into the woods on her own. But who could go with her?

Mel.

Pushing all thoughts of their argument to the back of her mind, Lauren ran to the farmhouse. Mel might be cross with her but this was an emergency.

Stumbling into the kitchen, she grabbed the phone and punched in next door's number.

'Hello?' Mel answered.

'Mel, it's me,' Lauren said urgently.

'Oh, hi.' Mel's voice was cold and Lauren felt a sudden flicker of doubt. What if Mel was so annoyed with her that she refused to help?

'Carly and Anna have taken Twilight

into the woods,' Lauren blurted out, her
heart beating wildly as she wondered
how she was going to persuade Mel to
help. 'I'm going to have to go after them
and help them get home safely. There's no
one else here and well, I –'

'Do you want me to help?' Mel
interrupted her, the frostiness vanishing
instantly from her voice. 'I'll come over
straight away and we can go together. I'll
bring Shadow and Sandy. It'll be much
faster if we go on horseback.'

Relief rushed through Lauren. 'Oh,
thank you. Thank you so much!'

'Get a torch and a flask of hot
chocolate,' Mel instructed. 'And write
your dad a note so he knows where

we've gone. I'll see you in a minute!'

Lauren quickly did as Mel had said. While the kettle boiled, she wrote a note saying they'd gone into the woods and then she found a torch and shoved it into a rucksack. She also added a blanket and a couple of extra scarves.

She was filling the flask when she heard a knock on the window. Mel was outside with Shadow and Sandy. Grabbing the bag, Lauren hurried outside.

'I've got some biscuits, two hand warmers and a first-aid kit,' Mel told her. 'I rang Jess and she said it's fine to take Sandy.' She threw Sandy's reins to Lauren. 'Come on! Let's go!'

Lauren scrambled on to the palomino's back and they cantered down the path.

'How long have they been gone?' Mel shouted through the swirling snow.

'About half an hour I think,' Lauren replied breathlessly, screwing up her eyes against the stinging snowflakes. 'But they might have been gone longer.' She explained about leaving them with Twilight while she went to help her dad.

'Which way do you think they would have gone?' Mel asked, reining Shadow in as they came to a fork in the path.

'I bet they took the main trail,' Lauren said. She wished she had Twilight. He would have understood that they were trying to find Carly and Anna and would have helped them follow their tracks.

They trotted down the left-hand fork. Sandy's hooves slipped and the young pony stopped uncertainly. 'Come on, boy. It's OK,' Lauren said.

She could tell Sandy didn't like the icy ground. 'We'd better just take it slowly,' she called to Mel.

They walked on, the ponies' hooves sliding every now and then in the snow. Lauren's fingers and toes got colder and colder despite her gloves and thick socks.

'What if they didn't come this way?' Mel said after a while.

'They must have. They wouldn't have gone down the narrow track,' Lauren pointed out.

'They might,' Mel said.

They halted the ponies and looked at each other uncertainly.

'What shall we do?' Lauren asked.

'Maybe we should turn round,' Mel suggested.

Lauren was about to agree when, all of a sudden, her eyes caught sight of four long silvery hairs caught on a bramble

that was sticking out into the path.
'Look!' she exclaimed. 'They look like
hairs from Twilight's tail! They must have
come this way.' She rode over and pulled
the hairs off the bramble.

'We don't know they're Twilight's,' Mel
said uncertainly. 'They could be any grey
pony's.'

'No,' Lauren said, shaking her head and
looking at the hairs in her gloved hand.
'I'm sure they're Twilight's. We've got to
keep going, Mel!'

To her relief, Mel didn't argue. 'OK,'
she said. 'Come on.'

They clicked their tongues and rode
on. Lauren scanned the track ahead. It
was hard to see through the swirling

snowflakes. Sandy's head drooped and she edged nearer to Shadow's side. Patting her neck to encourage her, Lauren felt a flicker of despair. How were they ever going to find Twilight, Carly and Anna? The woods were so deep and vast. Twilight could be anywhere – down a dead-end trail, near the quarry . . .

Just then a tree loomed up out of the snow in front of them. Sandy stopped with a snort.

'We've ridden off the main track,' Mel said. She looked around. Her face was worried. 'If we're not careful, we're going to get lost, Lauren. I really think we should go back and get help.'

Lauren hesitated.

'Come on,' Mel urged. 'We can't risk getting stuck out here ourselves.'

Part of Lauren knew Mel was right but she couldn't bear to turn round. Her friends could be in real trouble. She put her hands to her mouth. 'Twilight!' she shouted desperately. 'Carly! Anna!'

Shadow lifted his head and whinnied too.

There was a moment's silence. Lauren's heart sank. They were going to have to turn back. Mel was right. If they got lost, then there would be no one to get help . . .

Suddenly her thoughts were interrupted by a faint answering neigh.

Lauren would have known that sound

anywhere. 'Twilight!' she gasped. 'Come on, Mel! He's nearby!'

They headed in the direction of the whinny, weaving in and out of the snow-covered trees, their eyes peering through the blizzard.

'Twilight!' Lauren shouted again.

There was another answering whinny

and suddenly, just down the track,
Lauren saw Carly and Anna and Twilight
sheltering under the branches of a huge
fir tree.

'Lauren!' Anna shouted. 'We're over
here!'

Lauren touched her heels to Sandy's
sides and trotted over. Carly was holding
her wrist.

'Are you OK?' Lauren asked, jumping
off.

'I've hurt my wrist.' Carly was
shivering. 'Oh, Lauren, I'm so glad to see
you. We're lost!'

'We didn't know what to do,' Anna
said. 'Carly's wrist was hurting so much
she couldn't get back on Twilight and I

was too scared to ride him. I was going to come for help but I thought I might get even more lost and Carly didn't want me to leave her on her own.'

'What happened?' Mel demanded.

'It started to snow and Twilight didn't seem to want to go any further,' Anna explained, her voice trembling. 'Carly was riding him and he just kept stopping.'

'I tried to make him go on,' Carly said. 'But he threw his head in the air so I got off to lead him. I was trying to lead him along the path when I slipped on some ice and fell and hurt my wrist.' She looked like she was about to cry. 'I'm really sorry, Lauren.'

'It doesn't matter,' Lauren said.

'You look freezing,' Mel said to Carly.
'Here, we've got some hot chocolate and
some hand warmers.' She dismounted and
started pulling things out of her rucksack.

'I'll go for help on Twilight,' Lauren
said, shrugging off her own backpack and
handing it to Mel.

Mel nodded. 'Good idea. I'll stay with
Carly and Anna.'

'Oh, thank you, Mel!' Carly burst out.

'Do you mind staying?' Anna asked her.

'Not at all,' Mel answered. She looked
at Lauren. 'Go on!'

Jumping on to Twilight, Lauren turned
and they made their way carefully
through the trees. Carly and Anna were
both looking really pale and cold and she

knew she had to get help quickly. As
soon as she was out of sight, she
dismounted and said the Turning Spell.

In a flash, Twilight was a unicorn. 'I'm
sorry, Lauren,' he blurted out. 'I tried to
get them to turn back but they just kept
making me go on.'

'It's OK,' Lauren said. 'Come on, let's
go and fetch my dad. It will be quicker if
we fly.' Taking off her heavy jacket and
hat Lauren leapt back on. Twilight flew
up into the treetops. The snow was falling
faster than ever and Lauren could hardly
see through it.

A tree loomed up out of the snow.
'Look out!' Lauren cried.

Twilight swerved just in time. 'Sorry,'

he gasped. 'I can't see very well.'

He weaved in and out of the trees.
Lauren clung on tightly. It was a very
uncomfortable ride. Snowflakes hit her
face, catching on her eyelashes and
blinding her. Her skin felt numb with
cold. She remembered what Mrs Fontana
had said about flying through the snow.
'It'll be a wonderful experience,' the old
lady had told her. 'You won't forget it.'

Mrs Fontana must be mad, Lauren thought. *This isn't wonderful at all. It's dreadful!*

Twilight changed direction and then changed direction again. He slowed down uncertainly.

'What are you doing?' Lauren demanded. 'Come on, Twilight. Fly faster! We've got to get help.'

'I'm not sure where we are,' Twilight replied. He shook his head. 'I . . . I think we're lost.'

'Lost!' Lauren echoed. 'We can't be!'

'But I really don't know where we are,' Twilight said, flying down to the forest floor.

Frustration welled up inside Lauren.

This couldn't be happening. Carly and Anna needed her to get home, to get help. 'For goodness' sake, Twilight!' she cried. 'You're a unicorn! You're supposed to have magic powers. How come you can't even fly through a snowstorm?'

'I'm sorry, but I just don't know how,' Twilight said unhappily.

Lauren thought of her friends in the cold and lost her temper. 'This is so stupid!' she shouted.

'Lauren!' Twilight protested, stamping a front hoof in the snow.

At once a purple spark flew up from the snow and hovered in front of his nose. Twilight snorted in surprise.

'What's that?' Lauren said, astonishment

making her forget her anger.

'I don't know.' Twilight peered at the
spark. The air around it was shimmering
in a pale violet circle that got bigger and
bigger as they watched. 'It feels warm.'

Lauren's eyes opened wide. 'Look at the
snow around it!'

As the snowflakes touched the edge of
the violet light, they vanished, so that
there was no snow falling inside the
circle.

Lauren and Twilight stared. What was
going on?

CHAPTER
Ten

'The purple spark is melting the snow!' Twilight exclaimed.

'It must be one of your secret unicorn powers,' Lauren said. 'Quick, stamp your hoof again.'

Twilight stamped his hoof in the snow and another spark flew up. It hovered over his ears, and instantly snow stopped falling on his head.

Twilight stamped again and again. Soon
there was a whole line of sparks arching
over him and Lauren. Their shimmering
violet glow melted the snowflakes so that
they could see ahead, and kept them dry
and warm inside the circle.

'Oh, Twilight!' Lauren gasped. 'This is fantastic. Now we'll be able to find our way home.'

Twilight plunged into the air. The late afternoon sky was dark now, but the arch shimmered above him like a rainbow. Lauren felt warmth flow through her as they cantered high in the sky. It was amazing to be able to canter through the falling snow without it touching them.

She looked up and saw the magic rainbow arching overhead, a mass of glittering, shiny sparks. Her skin seemed to tingle and glow. It was like being in a magic bubble, just her and Twilight, separated from the world. She stroked his smooth warm neck and watched the snow flash by.

'I know where we are,' Twilight said suddenly. 'We're not far from home. Hold on tight!'

Lauren gasped in delight as he swooped through the snow so fast that the winter sky blurred lilac around her. The wind streamed through her hair and she laughed out loud. Suddenly she understood what Mrs Fontana had meant about flying in the snow. She knew she would never forget this. Not ever!

In less than five minutes they were at the edge of the woods. Twilight flew to the ground and Lauren quickly turned him back into a pony. They galloped out of the trees and up the path.

Her dad was hurrying out of the house, the keys of the Land Rover in his hand. Lauren guessed he had seen her note.

'Dad!' she shouted. 'Carly and Anna are in the woods. Carly has hurt herself! Quick! They need help!'

It didn't take her long to explain what had happened. Mr Foster got into the Land Rover and followed her into the woods. Sure-footed as ever, Twilight cantered along the track until they reached the tree where Carly, Anna and Mel were sheltering.

Lauren was relieved to see that some colour had come back into Carly and Anna's cheeks. Mel had made them wrap

blankets round their shoulders and had
shared out the hot chocolate and biscuits.
With hand warmers to keep their hands
warm and the spare scarves round their
necks, they looked much more cheerful.
Mel had even put a bandage from the
first-aid kit on Carly's injured wrist.

'Mel's been fantastic!' Carly called to
Lauren as she reined Twilight to a halt
beside them.

'Absolutely brilliant!' Anna agreed. 'It
would have been awful staying in the
woods on our own.'

'You've done a great job, Mel,' Mr
Foster said. 'Well done.'

Mel smiled. 'No problem. I was just
glad I could help.' Lauren beamed at her,

hoping her friend could tell how grateful she was.

'Come on,' Mr Foster said to Carly and Anna. 'Let's get you back to the farmhouse.' He gently helped Carly to her feet.

Carly looked at Lauren. 'I . . . I'm really sorry we brought Twilight out into the woods and caused so many problems, Lauren.'

'It's OK,' Lauren told her as she helped Carly along.

'We wanted to prove to you we weren't useless,' Anna said. She bit her lip. 'I guess we didn't do that.'

Lauren frowned. 'But I don't think you're useless.'

'You do,' Carly said. 'You won't even let us muck out.'

'But you don't like it,' Lauren said. 'You keep going on about how dirty and smelly and cold it is.'

'We don't really mind it,' Anna said. 'It was just a bit of a surprise at first.'

'And you were worried about getting mud on your jeans,' Lauren reminded Carly.

'Only my new jeans,' Carly told her. 'I don't mind getting my old jeans dirty.'

'Oh,' said Lauren.

Mr Foster looked at them. 'It sounds to me like there's been a bit of a misunderstanding.'

'We've just been feeling really dumb,'

Carly said. 'At least, compared to you, Lauren.'

Anna nodded. 'You know so much now about horses and the countryside. We thought you might not want to be our friend any more.'

Lauren swallowed. 'I guess I do know different stuff now,' she admitted. 'But you're still my friends.' She looked at them. 'And you'll always be my friends.'

The two girls looked very happy.

'Really?' Carly said.

'Really!' Lauren promised, amazed they could have thought otherwise.

The next minute they were all hugging.

'Ow!' Carly gasped as her wrist

knocked into Lauren's back.

'Come on,' said Mr Foster. 'I think it's time we went home. Lauren, will you and Mel bring the ponies back?'

Lauren nodded.

Mr Foster started the Land Rover and drove slowly away. Carly and Anna waved out of the back window until they vanished round a bend in the track.

Lauren and Mel got back on to Twilight and Shadow and, with Mel leading Sandy, they set off through the trees.

Lauren glanced at her friend. 'Thanks for helping, Mel,' she said quietly.

'That's OK,' Mel replied. 'I'm relieved that they were both all right – and Twilight too, of course.'

Lauren felt a rush of gratitude. 'I'm sorry we argued, Mel,' she said impulsively. 'I really did mean to ring you back yesterday, I just forgot.'

'I shouldn't have made such a big deal out of it.' Mel sighed. 'I guess I was just feeling a bit jealous. It was weird seeing you with other friends – other best friends.' She looked down at Shadow's mane.

Lauren hesitated. 'Carly and Anna are my best old friends and I still really like them, but you and Jess are just as important. You're my best *new* friends.' She looked at Mel. 'Is that OK?'

To her delight, Mel looked happy. 'Yes,' she said. 'It is.'

They smiled and rode on.

'Well, I guess you'll be busy with Carly and Anna tomorrow,' Mel said when they reached her house. 'So I'll see you on Christmas Eve.'

Lauren had a sudden idea. 'Or you and Jessica could come over to my house tomorrow,' she suggested. 'If the weather's better, I'm going to take Carly and Anna to this secret clearing I found in the woods. We could all go together and then in the afternoon we could get the ponies ready for the show.'

'OK,' Mel said. 'I'll see you tomorrow then.' She clicked her tongue and rode Shadow towards the fields. 'You know,' she said, looking round and grinning, 'maybe Carly isn't that bad after all.'

Lauren grinned back. 'See you tomorrow!' she said and she rode away down the drive.

The snow had stopped now and as she rode through the silent white world Lauren finally understood what Mrs Fontana had meant about all friends being important – old friends, new friends and special friends. She wanted – and needed – them all. Suddenly, Lauren realized she had one more apology to make.

She turned Twilight into the copse of trees at the side of the road and said the words of the Turning Spell.

With a flash, Twilight turned into a unicorn. 'Oh, Twilight,' Lauren said. 'I'm really sorry I lost my temper in the snow. I wasn't really angry with you.'

'It's OK,' Twilight told her. 'You were just worried about your friends. And now we've discovered how much fun flying in the snow can be!' He blew on her hands. 'It hasn't been an easy week for you, Lauren.'

Lauren's heart swelled. She'd hardly had any time to spend with Twilight over the last few days, but he had never once got cross or upset with her. 'I love you,' she told him, stroking his mane. 'I've hardly had any time for you, but you've never stopped being my friend.'

'I couldn't,' Twilight said simply. He nuzzled her. 'I'm your unicorn, Lauren. That means we're friends forever.'

Lauren's eyes prickled with happy tears. 'Forever,' she whispered, hugging him.

CHAPTER
Eleven

The next morning dawned without a cloud to be seen in the bright blue sky. The snow sparkled like diamonds in the gentle winter sun. Mel and Jessica came over at ten o'clock and the five girls set off to the clearing. On the way there they kept trading places so everyone got to ride. Even Carly, whose sprained wrist had been strapped up by the doctor, managed to get on Twilight and have a trot.

'I can't believe I never even knew this track was here,' Mel said as Lauren took them down the narrow overgrown path.

'It's a bit spooky,' Jessica said, looking at the tall trees with their bare snow-covered branches pressing in at them.

'Yeah,' Anna agreed. She shivered. 'It feels like there might be ghosts or . . . oh wow!' She gasped as the track led into the clearing.

The moonflowers had pushed their star-shaped heads through the snow so that the grass looked like a white carpet dotted with purple stars. A pair of robin redbreasts were flying across the clearing.

They landed on a nearby bush and
chirruped at the girls with their heads on
one side. A red squirrel crouched on the
snow-covered grass mound in the centre
of the clearing. With a flick of its russet
tail, it scampered across the snow and up

a tree trunk. The snow was heavy on the branches and the air had a strange mysterious feel.

Lauren looked at her friends. Their eyes were huge in wonder.

'What an amazing place,' Carly whispered.

'It feels like . . . like it's magic or something,' Mel breathed.

Anna nodded. 'Like something weird could happen.'

'I love it,' Jessica said softly.

Lauren stroked Twilight's neck. She'd been wondering if she was doing the right thing by bringing her friends to the clearing, but now she was very glad she had. The clearing seemed even more wonderful with all her friends there to share it.

They stayed for a while and then, leaving the clearing to the squirrel and the robins, they headed back to the farmhouse. Mrs Foster was waiting with a delicious brunch of pancakes, hot chocolate and Christmas muffins.

After brunch they got the ponies ready for the show.

'I'm going to miss being here,' Carly said as she helped Mel wash Shadow's tail.

'You'll have to come back,' Mel said.

'Yeah, when it's warmer,' Jessica put in. 'Then we can all go out for a picnic.'

'Or if you came at Easter, we could go

for an Easter-egg hunt,' Mel said.

'Cool!' Anna said. 'Can we do that, Lauren?'

'Of course,' Lauren said happily. 'That would be great!'

The next day, Carly and Anna were up early with Lauren. They helped her muck out and give Twilight a final brush over before the show. They has just finished decorating his bridle with tinsel when Anna's dad arrived.

There was a flurry of activity as they loaded up their holdalls and thanked Lauren's parents. Then Carly and Anna got into the car.

'Good luck at the show!' Carly called.

'Phone us and tell us how it goes,' Anna said.

'I will,' Lauren promised. 'See you at Easter!'

She waved them off and five minutes later Mel's mum arrived in the horse box with Mel and Jessica.

'Hi, Lauren!' Mel shouted, winding down the window.

'Are you ready for the show?' Jessica cried.

Lauren grinned. 'You bet!'

Despite their disastrous practice on Monday, Mel, Lauren and Jessica won five team rosettes in the show – a fourth in the bending, a third in the potato race, a second in the walk, trot and gallop and two firsts in the sack race and the relay. In fact, they won so many rosettes that they were awarded the prize for best team aged ten years and under.

After they had each been presented with a small silver shield, they galloped round the indoor arena with the tune of 'We Wish You a Merry Christmas' booming out through the loudspeakers. Lauren didn't think she'd ever felt happier. She could see it was starting to snow again outside, it was Christmas Day tomorrow and she had the best friends in the world – old ones, new ones and, of course, one very special one.

When they rode out of the ring, Mel

and Jessica went over to Mel's mum, but Lauren reined Twilight in. Listening to the Christmas music playing in the background, she dismounted and hugged him.

Twilight snorted softly.

Lauren kissed his neck. Even though he wasn't a unicorn right then she knew just what he was saying.

'Merry Christmas to you too, Twilight,' she whispered.

For a moment they stood there with snowflakes falling all around them and then, smiling happily, Lauren led him over to join the others.